Why am I doing this?

By Anne Holley

Hope you enjoy my book
Anne Holley

Published by New Generation Publishing in 2022

First Edition

ISBN: 978-1-80369-310-1

www.newgeneration-publishing.com

New Generation Publishing

All proceeds from this little book go to charity!

My thanks for all the help! Doreen and Judith for their support...

and Tim Wander for his advice and pulling this little book together!

Why am I doing this?

By Anne Holley

Contents

This little book is a light hearted account of how Rosie takes on challenges to raise money for her local charities.

Testing her courage, determination, sheer strength of character and most importantly her sense of humour. A selection of five stories which I hope will have you laughing from beginning to end.   Please enjoy.

Anne Holley.

SEWING..SEWING....AND........MORE SEWING

A bride first methinks to really have that "WOW" factor
and hopefully gets everyone's attention

Each stitch is sewn so neatly with hands that show signs of arthritis, concentration from faces that have experienced much, eyes that need glasses, but the end result is exquisite .....so much talent, this got me thinking....

Let me explain myself, my name is Rosie, I am the hairdresser at our local Day Centre. Finishing my work early and sitting in on one of their craft afternoons, I was amazed at the wealth of talent around the table. Knitting, Crochet, Embroidery, Cross stitch, making clothes for young and old, the list is endless.......

One weekend having a clear out at home, I found my daughter's discarded walkie talkie doll. Asking first to make sure she didn't want it, I decided to put it to the ladies, would anyone like to dress her for a raffle prize. Two ladies, Alice and Ivy, immediately showed interest and volunteered.

My head then went into overdrive

'What if I was to get a supply of dolls, materials, etc, and we had a dolls exhibition to raise funds for the day centre.

'Yes, yes' came excited replies from everyone, lets begin

Lists were made, ideas in abundance, offers of 'Ive got some material', 'Ive got some trimming, 'Ive got some flowers for their hair' and so on.....

I'm sure I heard them say "Hello please take me home with you?"

My first job was to make a list of toy manufacturers in England, eager to fly the flag and place an order.

Full of hope I started to ring round, only to fail at the first hurdle, working down my list I was repeatedly told 'sorry I cannot help you',dialling my last call and feeling despondent that no-one could help me, I spoke to a very nice man, who unfortunately informed me that I would not get a 'Made in England' doll, he was the last factory to make them, a few years ago. How sad is that, hmm, now what do I do?

Putting the word around that I was stuck, a friend of a friend thought he knew someone who had a lock up in Wimbledon, of unsold stock, from anything to everything, certainly toys, would I like to take a look. Well, it was worth a trip

.

Trying not to get too hopeful, taking a girlfriend with me, we drove over the following Saturday. Shown into a large warehouse by the 'caretaker', my immediate thoughts 'oh heck, JUNK', you name it really was stacks of anything and everything. Being led over to the toy section my eyes were darting here and there, hoping 300 dolls would leap out at us. We sifted through mounds of 'stuff' for about 20 minutes when eventually we honed in on a doll.

PERFECT……….WOW

About 20 inches high, nice figure, pretty and with long blonde hair. Almost unable to contain myself I tentatively asked the man if by chance he had any more.

I pegged the finished dresses up so they wouldn’t crease.

Scratching his head and looking thoughtful 'Well, I have no idea, it is a long time since anyone has shown any interest in this lot, I only keep an eye on things for everyone. You are welcome to go through it all, take your time, I am here all day. I shall be in my office in the far corner, shout if you need any help'.

After about an hour, we noticed right at the back, stacked up against the wall a considerable amount of boxes of varying sizes.

'Do I dare think that dolls could be inside'? I tentatively asked my friend with fingers crossed.

No sooner said we were clambering over like two women possessed, lids off and there staring up at me, were pretty faces with bright blue eyes, I'm sure I heard them say 'hello, please take us home with you'. Doing a quick count up at least hundred dolls, WOW, what an amazing find.

Different size boxes were unearthed containing smaller dolls, all of which we put in a pile. With heaps of energy, constant chatter and help from the 'caretaker' we yanked all the boxes out, my goodness me, over two hundred dolls. Decision time, do I go for it, or play safe… **GO FOR IT!!**

.....so we took the dolls out of their comfy boxes and transferred them into bin liners. 'Sorry girls I promise you, you will have exciting times to come and beautiful clothes to wear'.

Price negotiated, we loaded them into the car, having just enough room to shut the doors (good job it was an estate car), everyone happy, we drove off. I was on such a high my head nearly went out of the sunroof.

'We can do this, do that, so many different designs of outfits, colours........ oh heavens I just want to get started!! such was my conversation on the way home.

Garage doors open, the 'girls were stacked up in the corner, just giving enough room to park my car

Needless to say I didn't sleep a wink that night, thinking of all those pretty dolls in my garage, imagining them all fitted out with ball gowns, wedding dresses ......etc.

Next morning I was on an adrenalin run, up early, ready to begin, good job it is Sunday and I didn't have work, I started measuring up making a basic pattern for each size of doll, these in time were renewed many, many times, through much use.

I only work four days, so tomorrow (Monday) a trip to the market, meanwhile sort my upstairs 'spare' room out, set up my sewing machine and oil it, do a count up on needles, pins, cottons, etc., and make that list.

First thing next morning I was up and out, Kingston market here I come. Although crowded, which usually is a no, no for me, I headed straight for the materials. My goodness me I was like a child in a sweet shop. Every

colour and shade under the sun, reds, blue's, green's, yellow, pink, plain, patterned, flowered, checks and so on. Having decided I would buy the material in 3 metre lengths, I proceeded to pick up an assortment, and of course the all important white 'satin', lace and netting for the brides.
By the time I had finished, about 30 different materials, I moved onto trimmings, cottons and decorative flowers, for the finishing touches. This became a regular trip and I soon got to know the people, who very kindly always gave me a discount.

Once home, coffee, and a quick sandwich, I cannot wait to get started, the excitement and adrenalin taking over. A bride first methinks to really have that 'WOW' factor and hopefully get everyone's attention.

Within a few days we were 'up and running', my girls Alice and Ivy' set to work finishing 3 dresses each every week, but I was soon under pressure, by 'them' to do more, so ……once home, completing the basics in life like washing, ironing, housework and yes feeding myself, I was working full steam up in my room.
Rigging up lines across my work room, I pegged the finished dresses up so they wouldn't crease, this also helped me to make sure colours and designs were varied.

In my head I had this very colourful picture of my beautiful dolls, giving everyone the 'WOW' factor when they came into the exhibition, I wasn't going to disappoint myself, and more importantly my 'girls,' by having too many duplicate dresses. It was decided that I would pay them some 'pocket' money for all their hours of hard but enjoyable work, so everyone was happy.

While doing my 'official work' at the Day Centre interest grew, people came into my room with material, dolls of all shapes and sizes, buttons, poppers, lace trimmings, you name it anything to do with sewing, even an evening dress for me to cut up, the support was amazing, hairdressing seemed to be an after thought. Several weeks later going into my room to start work, a pile of first size knitted and crocheted baby clothes in pastel colours had been donated, again exquisitely done, perfect for my 'baby' dolls.

With almost enough dresses made, I started working on the dolls hair, some even going under the hairdryers, much to the amusement of my 'real' clients. I think it was talked about in the dinning room, people were forever 'popping' into my room to see what I was up to. A big oversight by me 'packaging', a lady came into see me, asking if she could buy a doll before the exhibition as she was sending it to America.

'Of course you can' then it struck me, I hadn't given it a thought as to what I was going to put the dolls in.

'Board meeting girls, emergency!!! what do we do'?? lots of suggestions thrown around, we then came up with the idea of a material bag with a draw string….. great, now I have some 'extra homework', 300 bags with a drawstring, problem solved, well almost!! Another trip to the market for what seemed a mile in length of different coloured lining material and tape for the bags.

The time had come to make arrangements, dates, venue and what was needed for our exhibition.

Our Day Centre was in a beautiful old Victorian house in its own grounds, the clients use the downstairs, while myself and the office staff use the upstairs. I was able to book the second lounge upstairs, which was only used for meetings, perfect for size and light as it had windows on two walls, making it a light and airy room, even on a grey day.

Booking myself out from work one afternoon, Alice and I started dressing the dolls, we were like a couple of little girls at Christmas, excitement, chatter and lots of cups of tea.

Taking a doll out of a bin liner I held it up and said

'Oh look a reject she has odd legs'..... a few seconds later

'Thank you Rosie' came a small voice from across the room. Realisation of what I said gave me total embarrassment, my face went crimson, I stuttered an apology, Alice has an artificial leg, having had amputation from a serious illness. This is so strange because I see her as a 'whole' person and never give a thought that she has a disability. She then enjoyed my discomfort, stared at me for a couple of seconds and burst out laughing, phew!! both laughing together, time for another cup of tea methinks.

I can remember doing some shopping for her when she was unwell, taking it into her she was in her wheelchair, without her artificial leg, she saw my look of shock, 'Its okay Rosie everyone reacts like that, I see it as a compliment that I am seen as 'normal' and complete'.

This has come up in my work several time. One of my clients had polio at the age of nine months, because of this she used callipers and crutches throughout the years. Later on in her life she had to make a horrendous decision, because the crutches had damaged her shoulders, her doctor's stern advise to her, discard them and use a wheel chair, once made she knew from that day onwards she would never be upright again.

Many times she had to correct people, just because she was sitting in a wheelchair they tended to talk 'down' to her and be patronising.

'I might have a broken and disabled body but my mind is sound', by gum it was, right until she passed away in her eighties. I truly learnt much from her and Alice.

In fairness I do think people are embarrassed and don't know where to look, my thoughts, she like others desperately want to be seen as complete and whole, not too difficult .....methinks.

With trestle tables put up around the room, boxes as plinths to give height at the back, covered in white cloths the stage was set.

As we filled up the back of the tables the effect was gradually unfolding, what had been in my head for months was now taking shape. With all the large dolls in different poses, holding flowers and parasols, it was now time for the smaller dolls. They were an assortment, no more than twelve inches tall, thin, chubby, baby dolls, teeny boppers, you name it all shapes and sizes. Some were fun dolls so I sprayed their hair green, blue, red, all to capture little girls attention and perhaps to get Mums to buy.

Posters put up, an advert in the local paper, we were all set, the exhibition was on for a week. Of course being me I pictured the whole lot being sold, with demands of making more, but not so.

Having sold about half of the dolls, a decision to go to all the fetes and fairs was made, so off we went. This was interesting but sometimes frustrating with no sales, but, by the time Christmas came we had sold out, even the one I was going to keep for myself.

Although we made money for the Day Centre my greatest joy was Alice. Calling me downstairs to the car park one day, there in pride of place, a mobility buggy 'Alice's freedom transport'. No longer did she have to rely on the ambulance to pick her up and bring her to the Day Centre, or get some one to take her shopping. She had saved her 'wages' from her sewing, add-ed some money and now she had her wheels, my heart was full, she had a new lease of life ……..we hugged each other.

My boss came out to see us 'A job well done girls', we all heartily agreed, went inside for a much needed cup of tea and cake.

Oh my goodness this is it!!

LIFE MODEL

'Ready when you are Rosie' *came a kindly voice from the art teacher.*

Having been shown into a cupboard, yes it really is a cupboard, where all the art equipment is kept, an apology for such cramped conditions, I was asked to get ready, would I leave my clothes on the (dry) paint smeared stool. I glance up at all the overfull shelves about ready to topple, when my eyes fix on a painting of a man's face. He seems to be mocking me, I want to turn the painting round so he is facing the wall. With this thought I am shocked how 'off track' my thoughts are, but ....I do turn him round.

Shaking so much and fumbling with my buttons and zip with fingers that felt like dead sausages, I finally stood with my white house coat on, with the belt tied tightly around my waist, I am ready. Clothes in a neat pile with bra and knickers buried in the middle, in case an artist came in for more paper, I slowly pulled back the curtain.

My goodness, a room full of people, assorted ages, female and MALE!!! YIKES!! The end of the room where I was to stand had large wooden blocks that made up the stage, if extra staging was needed. The artists formed a horseshoe shape with their easels, so nobody's view was blocked, oh lorks, a new spasm of panic takes over, my body is trembling from head to foot. A few chairs scattered around the room, I suppose if they prefer to sit, hmm, maybe the shock of seeing my body, this might be necessary. After introductions which I could only mumble a reply as my lips felt as if I had had a double dose of Botox, I was asked what 'position' I would feel comfortable with, struck dumb, wanting to go into hysterics, which the teacher picked up on, a suggestion of my back to the class, holding onto the staging would give me security and comfort!!!, how thoughtful is that, more like a bottle of wine and I will do any position!!

Right, keeping silly thoughts out of my head I believe I have just been told 'we are ready Rosie'. Never, never will I complain about hot flushes, they are nothing compared to what I am experiencing now. I am shaking from head to foot, the sweat is pouring down my body, yes, it is sweat, not perspiration and I am certainly not glowing. Just do it Rosie they have pencils poised at the ready.

ONE.......TWO

THREE!

there, the housecoat is off and on the floor, my back to twenty or so artists all studying my body. My legs are shaking so much I grab the staging with both hands for fear of collapsing on the floor. No gasps of horror or disappointment came to my ears, no throwing of rotten eggs or tomatoes, jeers to get off go home etc....., in fact, it was.... Great proportions, look at her spine and from a dumpy middle aged woman, 'oh my goodness it is years since I have seen my hip bone like that, if ever'!!!

With more praise and nice comments I managed to quell the shaking, the sweat slowed down and started to dry, the only problem with this I felt itchy, not good when I am supposed to keep still. It is a most unusual feeling and situation, I think I could cope with a nudist beach where everyone is the same, nobody is taking any notice, but to stand in a room with thumbs and pencils held up, measuring my proportions, is weird to say the least.

The second part of the art class was to sit in a chair and pose, this was slightly better but now they are studying my front, oh lore........ my boobs are saggy, having breast fed two babies for six months each, doesn't do much for their shape. Now looking at my legs 'did I shave them' ...... will they notice the corn on my small toe......huh, bit late to worry now.......

All this running through my head when I am supposed to be relaxing...I do some yoga meditation which keeps me still for thirty minutes.

Class over everyone is packing up no, no, no, how do I pick up my housecoat gracefully when I am stark naked?? A caption must have popped up over my head, no sooner thought of when a lady came over and picked it up for me. I thanked her, she smiled and said I was good, wow, I needed one of those chairs, relief in abundance. With lots more 'well done Rosie' I scooted into the sanctuary of my cupboard, to get dressed.

Handing me a mug of tea through the curtain the teacher asked 'Will we see you next week Rosie 'mm... yes... okay' I mumbled,

How did I get into this ......well, doing voluntary work for our hospice on the Isle of Wight I became a pamperer doing manicures and hand massage. Wandering into the art room when I wasn't busy, I started talking to one of the helpers, conversation turned to the art class that she went to every week, telling me how desperate they were for a LIFE MODEL

My legs are shaking so much I grab the staging with both hands.

'NO WAY!! dream on, absolutely never in a month of Sundays'!!!!!

'The pay is good Rosie, great for your fundraising' she very calmly replied. This fundraising is for monies that I would like to make for the art room, to purchase whatever Kate needs for her work with the patients. So this conversation went on for a few weeks, after a lot of persuasion, banter from some of the patients, a slight hesitation, I was caught.

'Right see you next Monday'

PANIC, PANIC, PANIC I go home, strip off, look in the mirror 'GHASTLY' is the word I use. I try some poses which is even worse. How do I get into these situation's, at this moment in time I am starting a new life, will taking one's clothes off be the new path I go down.....

I suppose you could say it is very liberating!!

Counting the days .....six in all, I feverishly work out how much weight I can lose, toast without butter, sandwiches with scrape on, scrape off meat paste (yuck) a lettuce leaf with a squeeze of lemon, again yuck, that should get rid of my tummy.....

Get up early, on my step machine, 5,000 steps methinks, that's a good start, a breakfast of dry toast and black coffee. Walking boots on and a 10 mile walk, that should do the trick, a bit of discipline will do me good.

Now the outer casing, make a list:-

exfoliate
shave legs
manicure
pedicure
face pack
oil body
hair……?….?….?

Well that's a problem it is shoulder length with SILVER streaks, shall I dye it, low lights, high lights, go red, brown, blonde or green/ red/ blue, whichever seems to be the fashion at the moment……. No Rosie they are concentrating on your body, just decide on the day whether you will be more comfortable having it tied back, up, or carefree and in its natural state….. like your body. Better still ask the teacher, hmm, decision made.

On the morning, shower, wash hair, take extra time applying makeup... now what shall I wear….. N.. O.. T.. H.. I.. N.. G..!!!!! with that thought I go into a mega frenzy and burst out crying 'I CAN'T DO IT, I CAN'T DO IT, NO,... NO,... NO,!!!!

Right, stop being a cry baby, dry your puffy eyes Rosie, make a cup of tea and yes….. this is extreme circumstances, a large chunk of that chocolate cake I happen to have in the fridge.

Eating like someone possessed, shovelling and swallowing without chewing, having my 'chocolate fix' I feel calmer, my thoughts go to the reason why I am doing this HOSPICE, HOSPICE, HOSPICE,…… who cares if my tummy is rounded through cake, gives me character and a more lived in body, hmm...natural is the word that comes into my mind……..and so this is how it evolved….

The day after my first 'modelling' I was working in the day room where some twenty or so patients and staff were chatting. Sitting in front of my client, applying nail varnish, this very droll voice boomed out.

'Well, did you get your kit off yesterday Rosie'?

A few seconds of silence around the room, nail varnish brush suspended in mid-air, conversation dwindled to nothing, all faces turned to me, waiting for an answer.

YES came my simple reply.

The whole room fell about laughing and cheering, then came the comments.

'WE HAVE PAPER AND PENCIL, READY WHEN YOU ARE ROSIE'

That afternoon certainly was a hospice with a difference.

I am in fits of laughter, every time THAI takes a breath he has a wheeze

WETSUIT ANYONE?

Now what is going on, I am sitting in front of a client at the hospice, chatting away doing her nails, when my ears prick up at the sound of voices coming into the room, the end of the sentence ......wetsuits. With that they purposefully walk over to me.

'Rosie you are sporty, do you by any chance have a wetsuit?', asks our fundraiser.

'Yes I do, I wear it when I go kayaking, if anyone would like to borrow it, I believe it is a size 10-12, feel free, it is in good condition, I can pop it in tomorrow. 'That won't be necessary as you will be in it'.

'Huh' as I looked up with a puzzled expression, stopping what I was doing, by now the patients around me are listening in. 'We are doing a fundraising day at the Folly Inn in Whippingham and it involves DOGS.

Right, I am now interested, anything to do with dogs must be exciting and fun. 'Let me explain, we have 10 of the country's biggest dogs.... Newfoundland pedigrees, weighing in collectively at around 140 stone, to do a demonstration, rescue, and display of their amazing skills.......do I have your attention Rosie?

W O W !!!!! I am now really interested. 'Are you free in 2 weeks' time on a Saturday'?

‘Most certainly’ my thoughts, nothing will get in the way of this challenge, even though they haven’t given me any details, ‘what do I have to do’?

‘Basically you will be thrown into the Medina River and HOPEFULLY rescued by one of these dogs. Can you tread water?, then if all goes tits up can you SWIM?.....

‘Oh right, now we are getting to the nitty gritty. Yes, I am a pretty strong swimmer, I would love to do it’.

‘Go for it Rosie, we will sponsor you’, came a chorus of voices....

Once again I am badgering my friends for their money, loads of moans and groans ‘

‘Now what are you doing Rosie?’, asks my pal Carol, as they all dive into their wallets and handbags, handing over their pension, which I gleefully whip out of their hands and stuff in my fundraising pot.

‘Come to the pub on Saturday and all will be revealed’ says I.

The day arrived, beautiful sunshine, loads of spectators, I glance over to the other side of the car park, well, are they really classed as ‘DOGS’, they are HUGE!!!
No time to go over to them, I am told to get into my wetsuit, so off I pop to the ladies. Is there an easy way to get into these things?, being a warm day, I am working up a sweat and red in the face, how delightful. I am wanting to give over this cool and in control image, no chance, if the water is cool I

shall welcome it. Eventually, suitably attired, wetsuit, booties and buoyancy aid on, I join the group of volunteers. Listening to instructions, I am given a number, once it is called out, to make my way down the pontoon.

Lots of chatter, we all watch the first dog and human climb into the rib, complete with instructor and driver of the boat. A short spin out into the middle of the river, the rib then does a wide circle, instructions are obviously given and the 'drowning' person jumps in the water. The rib then does another wide circle, more instructions and in goes SQUIRREL the dog, hmm, not so sure about his name. Drowning person then lies back in the water, right arm stretched out, ready to grab the harness that Squirrel is wearing, hmm again, that seems pretty straight forward, human is towed back to the safety of the land. Squirrel then does a huge shake, sending water over everyone within a 10-mile radius, shrieks and laughter all round, people clap, raise their glasses, or wave a chicken drumstick that they are munching from the barbecue.

Well, my thoughts are 'that is all pretty straight forward' while musing I hear my number being called, right off we go. Stepping on to the rib I am introduced to THAI, that's better than Squirrel. I sit on the side of the rib, chat to the instructor then I turn my head sideways to look at Thai……he is sitting with his bottom on the floor of the rib, I am sitting on the side of the inflatable, a burst of laughter from me as our heads are the same height. He looks at me with an 'old fashioned' expression, his thoughts 'My goodness another hysterical female, perhaps I should leave this one in the water' I give him a hug trying to bond in the 10 seconds I have before my dip.
'Okay Rosie off you go', having thought's earlier of making an elegant dive, all that goes out the window, standing up I wobble, almost lose my balance

I give him a huge soggy cuddle and thank him for bringing me back safely.

and do a frog like entry into the water, CRIKEY!! this is refreshing, I think not!!! Turning so I can watch the boat, I suddenly feel very lonely in this big expanse of water, 'please don't forget me'........my head turns for a few seconds to glance at everyone enjoying themselves on the beach..... an engine noise comes to my ears, the rib has almost completed its circle and is about 50 metres away from me.

An instruction is given to THAI he gets up and does an enormous leap off the boat, I burst out laughing, he looks like a huge 'dumbo' covered with fur and from my low position in the water, flying high in the sky, with his fur splayed out making him appear twice his size, hmm, I think my auntie May had a fluffy hearth side rug once upon a time.......enough of that Rosie concentrate or you will miss your 'pick up'

Splash, with a mini tidal wave he is in, swimming like the clappers in my direction, again my laughter erupts, his head is going from side to side, eyes fixed firmly on me. At this point of no return I am not sure whether I am fodder for his next meal. Whew,... glad this is not Australia otherwise it could well be a shark 'H E L L O J A W S my what lovely teeth you have'!!!!

Come on Rosie Thai is working very hard with his 'doggy paddle' give him encouragement. Well, he has got some help, something I didn't know until today, Newfoundland's have 'web paws' like ducks have web feet, to propel him along, that's a thought, would be handy for us humans in times of drowning........my thoughts again, think of all those extra grapes you could crush if our.........stop it Rosie, be in the moment and don't let your mind wander....

All thinking stopped now as Thai is treading water, waiting for me to grab his harness, right arm out as instructed, I grab the red handle and he starts to tow me back to the beach. Again I am in fits of laughter almost taking in water and drowning myself, every time THAI takes in a breath he has this wheeze …. my goodness, I hope he doesn't conk out, should I be towing him I say.

All thoughts unfounded we reach the beach, and I am gently deposited on terra-firma, he does a huge shake, this time everybody is ready for him, they take a few paces back. I give him a huge soggy cuddle and thank him for bringing me back safely, he is not amused, resumes his bored look, job done, looks for his Mum and no doubt a treat for being a good boy.

This is going on all afternoon, much enjoyment by everybody, a photo shoot from my friends and our local paper, then I am ready to get out of my wetsuit. This indeed was the next challenge, I go into the ladies and spend 15 minutes trying to peel off this 'second' skin with no success, the more I try the angrier I became and hotter still. Luckily my cousin's wife Val, wondering if I was okay, came to the rescue. At the sight of me she bursts out laughing, we can do nothing until we control ourselves and take in the situation as serious. Eventually we managed, once showered and dressed, although still red in the face, with wet stringy hair, I looked presentable enough to go and have a meal.

A truly memorable day with much enjoyment, raising funds for the hospice as well.

'Rosie please look up and wave with BOTH hands for a photo shoot'.
Crikey!!
BLIP
BLIP

ROSIE'S ABSEIL

All-bran' no I don't think I shall need any for breakfast, now that the day for my abseil down the Spinnaker Tower has arrived, I am so full of nervous excitement.

A couple of weeks ago so not so, I parked my car at Seaview (this is on the Isle of Wight) assembled my fold up bike and cycled into Ryde to meet a friend for lunch.

It was a beautiful day, so on the way back I jumped off my bike, settled on the beach with my book to enjoy the rest of the sunshine.

This however was short lived, I glanced up, looked across the water to Portsmouth, there in the summer sunshine stood this majestic looking building, reaching up into the sky.

THE SPINNAKER TOWER

YIKES!! and lots of goose bumps, I shall be dangling from a rope on the outside of that building!!

Although the tower is 557 ft. high, I shall only be coming down 328 ft...... right..... no panic then!!

My calm and concentration gone, book forgotten, I went through a series of 'what ifs'.

What if they don't tie the rope properly?

What if the rope is too short and I am left dangling, would a fireman come and rescue me?

What if a gust of wind blows and I am swinging like a pendulum, TICK, TOCK, TICK, TOCK?

What if I am frozen to the spot like a rabbit when it is dazzled by headlights?

Doing a lot of pondering and hundreds of 'what ifs' over the next few days, the day has finally arrived, good advice has been given out in shedloads, one being that I must stop half way down, admire the scenery and listen, hmm, not easy as this 'OLE gal' will have removed her glasses and hearing aids, oh what a glamorous picture I make, thank goodness my teeth are well cemented in.

Right have I packed everything, water/smelling salts/spare socks/knickers/ phone/camera/ hairbrush/brandy and..... my lucky teddy bear.

My pal Diane is with me, I tell her to chatter on the way over to the ferry to keep my mind occupied, not that she needs encouragement, as she is certainly not a quiet petal.

Car parked, a brisk walk along the pier, I'm feeling quite bonnie, like the weather, it is a perfect day, sunshine and blue sky.

I'm on the ferry, somehow Diane has disappeared, I cannot see her 'WHERE IS SHE'? Getting twitchy and hot under the collar I ask the staff, no-one knows, then she appears 'I had to go to the loo Rosie S O R R Y !!.

JUST GET ON AND SIT DOWN,' came my stern reply, much to the amusement of fellow passengers. I do explain that she is only let out once a week, whereupon I receive a friendly thump, we are pals again.

The ferry moves off, the tower looms in the distance, my stomach doing somersaults, nervous chatter, almost hysterical as every second brings us closer.

Ropes tied up we have arrived in Portsmouth, a short walk, weaving our way through shoppers and holiday makers, we are now standing at the base of the tower. Having given ourselves plenty of time we find a seat nearby, craning our necks to watch the others do their descent.

I am now concentrating, hoping to learn a few techniques on the best way to ……DROP!! Amazingly each person seems to have their own version of abseiling, certainly the time it takes, varying from person to person.

Funny how some just happen to stop and HANG for a while …….wonder what all that is about …..having decided that I am going to be 'the' most professional and experienced 'at it', my eyes focus on a young man beckoning me over.

THIS IS IT!!

Giving Diane my glasses and hearing aids (perhaps been deaf and visually impaired might work in my favour), obeying instructions, I follow the young man to the entrance of the tower, he is talking to me but I am only hearing every other word, this is mainly down to my lack of 'ear extensions' but also my nerves have kicked in. Paperwork is handed to me but it is a blur without my glasses, so a lady fills it in, I sign, hopefully, on the dotted line.

Another young man appears, greets me with a lovely smile and points in the direction of the lift. I am doing this with another girl much younger than me who is, cool, calm and collected. On our way up I fire fifty thousand questions, he laughs, saying that all is well, but he can remember gluing something together that morning, but what it was escapes his memory. Had I not been trapped in a lift I would have 'legged it', more laughter from him, we arrive at the top, lift doors are opening.

Stepping out with wooden legs, we walk into a room resembling a conservatory

'Oh what a fantastic view.......it doesn't look that high up after all', I exclaim, full of renewed enthusiasm and energy. Ushered into the corner which is roped off for us abseilers, I am given a harness that seems slightly uncomfortable and unladylike, especially between the legs, hmm...... moving on, I am asked to put my hands on this young man's shoulders, my that's nice, until he gives a quick yank on the belt of my harness, making me gasp and gag for air, my waist measurement has gone from, well, a reasonable size to eighteen inches, wonderful, but I cannot BREATHE!! He doesn't seem worried and smiles.....next a large pair of heavy duty gloves are being handed to me.

‘Why such thick gloves?’ came my chirpy voice.

‘To stop the friction and heat from the buckle as you go down’ came a quick reply.

Gulping down air I could hardly comprehend that I would be going down so FAST!!

That completed I am directed to a door where I walk down two steps, hmm, that’s handy, a bit nearer to the ground, ‘every little helps as they say’.

Heavens we are right by the opening, a guy is waiting on the drawbridge to clip me on, my mouth is so dry my lips are stuck together.

A girl is waiting to give me a hard hat, my thoughts are ’if I drop 300 feet what good will it do’? I picture being concertinaed up inside the hat, with my eyes peeping out above the rim, with only my hands showing and waving‘

Right Rosie are you listening?’.... beaming me back from my erratic thoughts I am told to talk into the camera, which is on my hat. My reason for doing this...... why, no other than the Mountbatten Hospice on the Isle of Wight. My hat is then put on my head and the strap pulled firmly under my chin.

‘Hey you’ve caught a bit of Rosie’s hair with the strap’ shouts the ‘boy’ on the drawbridge. ‘AM I B-O-V-E-R-E-D’ I shouted with equal volume, at this stage of the challenge am I going to get in a tizzy about a bit of hair?’!!!!......

Now walking over to the opening I am given instructions, which have to be repeated twice, AGAIN!! I am clipped onto the wire by my belt 'that's it no escape', with uncontrollable shaking I am told to put both my hands on the wire, swing my left leg over and place my foot on the ledge.

'WHAT LEDGE!' I shouted, letting out a few expletives, for which I immediately apologise, the BOY grins and guides my foot onto the ledge. This ledge folks, I know I have big feet, is only the width of my trainer. I am then told to put my right foot behind my left, at this stage my foot won't behave, so the 'boy' does this for me. I cannot help but look down, my word, I am so high up, talk about a sheer drop, I put in a request

'Please may I have a parachute 'just in case?', another grin from the 'boy', he ignores my request, I am promptly given another instruction.

'That's fine Rosie now bend your legs and sit back into the harness, GEE WHIZZ!! NO, NO, NO, I'm sitting on nothing 300 feet up……where is the seat, armrests, cushions!! Oh dear, oh dear, a few more expletives, more instructions.

'Now, swing your left leg out, put your toe on the wall' I look to see if there is a ledge or foothold, nothing, so my trainer is just touching the wall, hmm….. methinks I am now like a monkey up a tree……

' Rosie are you listening'…..I am told to put my right foot against my left, GEE WHIZZ, BLIP- BLIP- BLIP!!

Talk about hanging by a thread, have you ever watched a spider making a web when he just seems to be hanging?, well that's me folks, first a monkey then a spider. I do ask at this stage whether I can have extra ropes, ONE rope doesn't seem strong enough, perhaps one around each ankle, wrists and at this point of no return my NECK!!......

Right, having been refused on all requests and assured that ONE rope is enough, I am instructed to put my left hand onto my belt and hold the rope with my right hand. WHOOPS!! BLIP BLIP HELP!!! BLIP BLIP I am lowered a few feet then told I am in CONTROL!!! BLIP BLIP 'I don't know what I am supposed to be doing', I shout.... BLIP BLIP. Now I cannot believe what I am hearing next....

'Rosie, please lookup and wave with BOTH hands for a photo shoot' CRIKEY!! BLIP BLIP what a thing to ask me, it was more a grimace than a smile, my arms and hands looked as if I was directing the traffic in Piccadilly Circus!!

Looking at the tower earlier the paintwork colours are fudge colour, white then blue, once I reach the blue I knew I would almost be down....

I was told to look around because the camera on my hat is working, but all that goes out the window. At one stage I panic and stop dead in my tracks, this FUDGE coloured paint goes on and on and on. I look up and down, methinks I am halfway, the drawbridge is 150 feet up, the ground150 feet below.......What the blue blisters do I do now.... think positive, do some deep breathing, if I can in this bloody straight jacket...........................

Stay calm........, I attempt to do yoga relaxation, working through my body which helps a bit. Oh my goodness me I still cannot move, I am trying to hug the wall, Rosie get a grip, this is a mental issue, you are perfectly SAFE, dangling from this rope. My thoughts then turn to all the patients in the hospice, who would dearly like to be in my place, this motivates me, with great effort to start my descent again.

I had thoughts earlier of turning round and shouting to Diane, 'does my bum look big in this', but all jokes were not possible, especially as my lips are still stuck together from having such a dry mouth, hmm, where has my saliva gone?

After a few minutes which seemed hours, my feet were touching WHITE paint, oh joy upon joy, I am making progress, now it won't be long until the blue appears. This keeps me going until my feet touch the ground, I am shaking from head to foot, a young man came over, unharnessed me, hat and gloves dis-guarded, I stand looking limp and sorry for myself .... OH NO!!! I burst into tears, how embarrassing is that. Young man says

'Would you like a hug'?

'YES PLEASE' says I with a pathetic voice and tear stained face. He then points me in the direction of another young man, who already has his arms wide open, hmm, I do a wobbly walk over to him and I am embraced. Hmm again, methinks he is employed as a professional hugger, for damsels in distress, how cute is that!

Young man say's 'would you like a hug?'

A booming voice from somewhere in the crowd, I believe to be from that delicate petal Diane, shouting above everyone else

' WELL DONE ROSIE'.

A photo shoot for the album I collect my video, upon inspection it consists of:-

FUDGE COLOURED PAINT
WHITE PAINT
BLUE PAINT

Now I know why I was told to move my head, I can multi-task but not when I am 300 feet up dangling from a rope.

This indeed was a challenge as I do not and still don't do heights, hindered or helped, I don't know, but my main thoughts were for our hospice on the Isle of Wight.

We have a 10 mile drop into the canyon, taking approx 7 hours. NOOOO!!!

GRAND CANYON

Right this is it, no turning back we are gaining speed up the runway, Las Vegas here we come. Can I really be flying so far just to be doing some walks, yes, is my answer. Having booked a 17-day trip with like-minded people, I am embarking on a strenuous walking holiday called Canyon Land.

I am equipped with all my walking gear and hopefully a 'fit' me, I settle back for a relaxing flight. Although I don't know anybody from my group, we are all sitting in the same area on the plane, and so obvious is our footwear that I didn't have to wonder if I had jumped on the right plane, we were all wearing our heavy walking boots to save weight in our suitcases, so by the time we arrive we have some knowledge of each other. My first thoughts, they are really serious walkers. Oh well I shall do my best.....

We have 7 stops on our tour, Cedar City, with Zion National Park. Bryce Canyon, Moab with their magnificent arches, Cortez with its delicate arch. The Mesa Verde Park with its archaeological sites, and Kayenta with its Monumental Valley. Last but not least the Grand Canyon. Although the walks were not particularly long, climbing out of the Grand Canyon for 14 miles, is the most challenging.

Goodness me, arriving at the Strat Hotel in Las Vegas I am absolutely spell bound, in a sort of ghastly way. Weaving our way through the casino (oh dear I am so naive, I have only seen scenes like this on the television), lights flashing, glasses and bottles of beer perched by the noisy machines.

I am, yes, horrified, so astonished am I that I gradually lag behind my group.

HELP!! unbelievably I'm lost in a hotel……

'Come on Rosie keep up otherwise you will get lost', shouted our leader.

Eventually I find my room on the 17th floor, having asked a fellow walker to knock on my door when we go down for dinner, no way can I find my way back to the restaurant. I pull back my curtains to be faced with a huge building that says 'TRUMP HOTEL' oh lore!!

We have a briefing that evening, again I am mesmerized at the amount of food, it is a self-servery from anything to anything. I watch as 'these people' consume more in one meal than we do for the whole day. This is the same at breakfast, no thank you, I will pass on the curry, pork chops, steak, Chinese, pasta dishes, gateaux, pies, any pudding you can think of, cake and pastries…….. Where are my cornflakes?…….

Our trip developed into an amazing adventure, never have I seen such sights, the vastness of the places, rock and sand, sand and rock. Wall to wall blue skies and sunshine, the temperature perfect for our walking.

At last we are at the Grand Canyon an air of excitement and trepidation, have I gained fitness or am I a tad worn out from the last 10 days hmm?….. we shall see in the next 2 days.

My fingers are numb, my legs are shaking, it is still quite dark, I can't stop my teeth from chattering, with frost still on the ground, it is very, very cold.

I am standing on the edge of South Rim waiting for us all to assemble. 'Pack light' we are told, looking down I have four layers of clothing on, 'take plenty of water please at least three litres, snack bars, suntan lotion, extra socks and most importantly SUN HAT!!!!, hmm 'this is packing light!!

Still feeling miserable I can hear our leader instructing us on our descent, safety measures, drink plenty of water even when you don't feel thirsty, keep to the inside of the path at all times, don't worry our pace will be slow, but sure.

This is my big challenge to walk from South Rim to North Rim of the Grand Canyon, with daylight approaching I can just make out the vastness of this huge canyon, looking down into it, it is so, so deep, somewhere is the Colorado River and our picnic stop, hmm if you say so……

I am fundraising for 'Ability Dogs for Young People', they train up puppy dogs to help any youngster with a disability, on the Isle of Wight, so I have lots of people who are supporting me, I mustn't let them down.

I have borrowed some walking poles from a friend, which at this moment in time, methinks are going to be a pesky nuisance, wished I'd left them at the hotel. We are starting to move off, a group of 'all-sorts', our age ranging from sixty-five to eighty, good grief, will I be doing this again at eighty, I think not!! We are chattering away about our challenge, what we think will be our experience's in our ten mile drop into the canyon. This will take approximately seven hours, tomorrow will be even longer, noooo, just don't go there, deal with the now and today first, please Rosie!!

The terrain as you can imagine is difficult to walk on, rock with a layer of loose stone, topped with a sprinkling of sand. Already my foot is slipping away from me causing me to unbalance slightly, this is very worrying as my usual walking rhythm cannot be achieved, already my calf muscles are beginning to create

Twisting and turning on the pathway, winding our way down we are seeing sensational views, how magnificent, with all the different rock formations and with the sun just coming up from behind the highest peak, throwing different colours onto the rocks, it is truly spectacular.

Stopping frequently for a glug of water, I give my calf muscles a quick massage, this helps especially as it is getting warmer, looking up I can see several walkers doing the same thing, this gives me comfort…….., well sort of!!!

Steps, shallow steps, giant steps, uneven steps, steps disguised by sand and stones, my goodness this is so difficult, no striding out on this walk.

Starting out at South Rim, Bright Angel Trailhead, we are 2085 m (6840 ft.) above sea level by the time we have walked just under half way, arriving at the ranger station called Indian Garden, we are1158 m (3800 ft.) quite a drop in under 8 km (5 miles).

I am doing alright, my toes feel a bit bunched up, my calf muscles still complaining, but we are having glimpses of the Colorado River, this cheers us all up.

I must admit I have been proved wrong about my walking poles, they are my best friend, keeping me steady on the most treacherous parts, giving me confidence and taking some of the pressure off my calf muscles. Thank you Tiena for insisting that I 'borrow' yours.

On a water stop we are given instructions on how to get the most out of our poles, correct level of our arms, position of our hands, and grip, last but not least we are not using them properly unless our wrists hurt.

'That's crazy' I comment!!

'Well' came our very knowledgeable leader 'better to have your wrists aching than your knees, you need them to get you up the top of North rim.

Hmm point taken!!!

Cheers from everyone, at last we have reached the Colorado River. Have we slipped into another day I ask myself, the sky is blue, the sun is warm, we are in shorts and tee shirts. Having tied my 'layers' around my middle I drop them to the ground, sit on a warm rock, eat my snack bars, and empty the last of my water bottles. Everyone has found their voices again, we are all happy and chatty (this reminds me of the days at school, on an outing).

Content with what I have achieved so far, this would be enough for me, pitch a tent by the river and spend the rest of the time here. We watch a few inflatables negotiate the fast swirling water then hear in the background a gentle but firm voice 'right everyone, time we moved on'.

We scan our eyes around the room,

Oh no we groan, ours are the top bunks!

Feeling energised and eager now to arrive at the Phantom Ranch, we quickly sort ourselves out, continuing along the path that runs alongside the river. Crossing a bridge and doing a photo shoot we are all in a better place mentally, our walking has more energy and meaning, a sense of purpose 'yes we will get there, not long now'.

About 4.30 in the afternoon the Phantom Ranch is in sight, cheers of relief, not long now to that much wanted shower!!! Upon arrival we are paired off and I pal up with Nicola, to be told that we are both in the end chalet, to sort ourselves out, dinner is at six thirty sharp.

We have now descended about 1300 m, 4265 ft. our ascent will be approximately 1700m, 5577ft. Hmmm.

Wearily we make our way along the walkway, open the door to our chalet, only to fix our gaze on bunk beds, 12 to be precise, assorted ruck sacks scattered on the floor and all the paraphernalia that us females carry around with us, scattered over the beds. In a slight panic we scan our eyes around the room to find two empty ones, oh no we groan, ours are both top bunks. Having no choice, we dump our stuff, quickly realise that now is the time to 'grab that shower', 12 females and 1 shower!!, no, no, no, we certainly don't want to be on the end of the queue.

Starting to strip off I look down at my trousers, they are disgusting caked in dust, but mostly from the knee down, luckily I have zips just above the knee to make them into shorts, so making an instant decision in two seconds, zips undone, the bottom part are being washed in my shower. Feeling human again my 'washing' is put outside to dry, I then make the

monumental decision to climb my ladder, to try out my bed. My calf muscles are really complaining, I feel like wooden tops, but eventually I flop onto my bed, 'wow' absolute bliss, at this point Nicola is warning me not to sleep as we only have twenty minutes before we eat, we have to be on time.
Little chance of sleeping, as within a few minutes, females of all ages burst through the door, returning to pick up whatever, prior to going in for a meal. Introductions made announcing our names, which I forget two seconds later, (not mine I hasten to add) and we are trundling off for our meal.

Entering a much larger chalet, we are confronted with rows of large tables that almost stretch across the room, with lots of wooden chairs, our group has the second table and we are seated. Large jugs of cold water are soon emptied and replenished, we are served homemade soup with a chunk of corn bread, delicious, eating as if we hadn't seen food for days, bowls empty and collected, we are then presented with very large pots of stew, gosh, this was out of this world, beef stew, so tender, with every vegetable you can think of including potatoes. Two helpings later feeling rather full I just about had room for a chunk of chocolate cake, goodness me, what a meal.

We had to leave the chalet then, so everything could be cleared away, but to come back at eight o'clock to have a drink. Having decided to do this we went back to our chalet. Only taking off my walking boots, leaving my trousers and hoodie on, I flopped onto my bed....

WHAT'S THAT NOISE!!! .... WHAT'S THAT NOISE!!!

‘Oh my word where am I’ lights switched on people moaning, assorted alarms going off from mobile phones, I am in total confusion…….

‘Don’t worry Rosie’ came a gentle voice from across the room, this was Nicola, reassuring me that it is four fifteen in the morning time, to get up. Oh for goodness sake that is obscene!!!! Apparently I zonked out at 7 30 not to be woken and here I am ready for my next day of challenges.

IT IS STILL THE MIDDLE OF THE NIGHT !!

Glancing across at the ‘young girls’ my goodness, they look absolutely beautiful, hair flicked back, eyes open wide, ready for the day. I can only half open my eyes, not see much because of my birds nest hair, with my face scrunched up because of the way I was lying in bed, in brief, a disgusting mess, Hey Ho!!! I very carefully descend down my ladder as my whole body aches now and won’t move properly, I hope I get a chance to do some stretching.

Ablutions completed, bags packed we are ready for breakfast (it is now five o’clock) yet again we eat masses of food, bacon, scrambled eggs, pancakes with maple syrup and loads of coffee. We are given pack ups which we quickly sort out, swap things or leave behind what we don’t want.

Assembled outside we are given instruction as to what to expect for the first part of our walk, apparently…... it is easy and fairly flat AT FIRST!! so... with an abundance of enthusiasm off we go. It is still dark so we are all carrying

torches, so necessary on this very uneven path. The day is waking up, we are blessed with blue skies and sunshine, our second breakfast is eaten about seven o'clock, everyone is chatty, relieved that we have day one behind us, no injuries or mishaps, so fingers crossed this will be the pattern of things, until we get to the top.
The first hour or so is pretty flat, walking alongside the creak and going over several bridges, after our third breakfast, and a couple of hours later, we start the ascent in earnest. I am using my poles, concentrating on my breathing, and with the sun beginning to warm up, I am now in shorts and tee shirt, and most importantly wearing my faithful sun hat.

By midday the sun is pretty warm, frequent water stops are a must, when we come to a loo stop, which I hasten to add are pretty dire, but so necessary, (not many trees in the canyon), a water tap to fill up our bottles 'yet again,' we set off as soon as we are ready, before stiffness creeps in.

I am now using my poles all the time, the paths are getting steeper, it is pretty hot, added to which the path we are following has closed in, the sun is bouncing off the rock to add to the heat. Walking for about five hours it is now around one o'clock, I am showing and feeling tiredness, my calf muscles are creating again 'come on Rosie', yesterday you were walking downhill all the time, now it is uphill, what do you expect!!!'

We sit on some rocks in the shade to enjoy the view and oh how cruel is this, a line of mules goes past taking their riders up to the top, we stop eating and drinking, all with the same thoughts 'if only'. Our leader honing in on us promptly says that if we cheated we wouldn't feel that we have achieved, how could we tell family and friends.......at this stage.........

I am hanging onto my poles for support, my new name 'MRS NO-LEGS',
we are all very weary.

EASY

We are up and on the path again, I glance up at the wrong time, see this long winding path ahead of us, that seems to go on for a million miles, up into the sky and beyond, oh gosh, at this stage I am seriously wondering whether I shall make it, I am at a very low ebb, a thought kicks in, I've got to, I have loads of people who believe in me and have sponsored me for my chosen charity. Right then, deep breathing,

'GET ON WITH IT'.

Our drink stops are more frequent, our leader, without saying anything realises that we are struggling, could also be that the pain killers are being popped by a few people more frequently, several are falling behind, a couple noticeably limping. What a sight we look, chatting is almost non-existent, all intent on completing the last couple of hours.

I am keeping my eyes down, just focusing on the next step ahead, my whole body is creating, to lift my leg up onto another step is just t...o...o.......much, I am relying heavily on my poles, so much so, not only do my wrists ache, but my arms neck and shoulders, had my knees had to take the load up each step, I do know that I wouldn't have made it. We now have about an hour's climb to the top, with added information 'is the toughest part' being steeper than what we have so far experienced, how cruel is that, well, no turning back, no cheating with a mule

GET ON WITH IT, AGAIN!!!!

(these few words are repeated time and time again)

I am now crying with exhaustion, good job I have my sun glasses on, no one can see me, surely it can't be much further, my legs really do not want to work. Gradually, with each laboured step, with an air of excitement, our leader is passing through to us that we are almost to the top, with deep breathing and calm me down yoga thoughts, I can see an opening through the trees, goodness are we really at the top, an almighty push with my sticks up the steep slope and we appear in an area where people have congregated after their walk, they are all clapping us.

I am hanging onto my poles for support, my new name MRS NO-LEGS, we are all very weary and just want our hotel and a bath. Cheers all round our coach has arrived only to see an official waving his arms about explaining that the coach couldn't stop there, we watch almost in tears as he drove off.

Eventually we boarded our coach but not before we had had to walk a mile to find it, once at the hotel I opened my bathroom door only to see a shower, oh well, who cares, I have just walked.................

RIM TO RIM OF THE GRAND CANYON

Next day all weary but content, we clambered onto the coach to make our way back to Las Vegas, to the Strat hotel. On entering the hotel, I am near to tears and panic, having experienced so much natural beauty for 2 weeks I cannot cope with fags, food, flashing lights and noise. Quickly scooting up to the sanctuary of my room I lie down on my bed and relive the last 2 days, amazing.

Ready now to eat, chat and 'people watch' we all enjoy the last evening of our amazing trip.

As it is our last night 4 of us went up to the revolving restaurant, thank goodness just for a drink, each cocktail was £16, CRIKEY, what would we of spent had we had a meal...........

Our flight next day was uneventful and quiet; I reckon we all slept most of the way content in the thoughts of what we had all achieved. Our leader was really pleased with us all, the year before 4 walkers dropped out, stayed in a hotel to wait.........huh, we are amazing!!

I would like to say thank you to everyone who sponsored me, also to thank Tiena who insisted, VERY FIRMLY that I borrow her walking poles, without them...........

ANNE HOLLEY

Born in 1951 I spent my school years in Mortlake Middlesex.

Moving to Shepperton with my family at the age of 14, I worked my apprenticeship as a hairdresser.

I have two children, four grandchildren and two great granddaughters.

Now retired my hobbies are walking, dancing and writing for charity.

Lightning Source UK Ltd.
Milton Keynes UK
UKHW050806141022
410463UK00010B/480

9 781803 693101